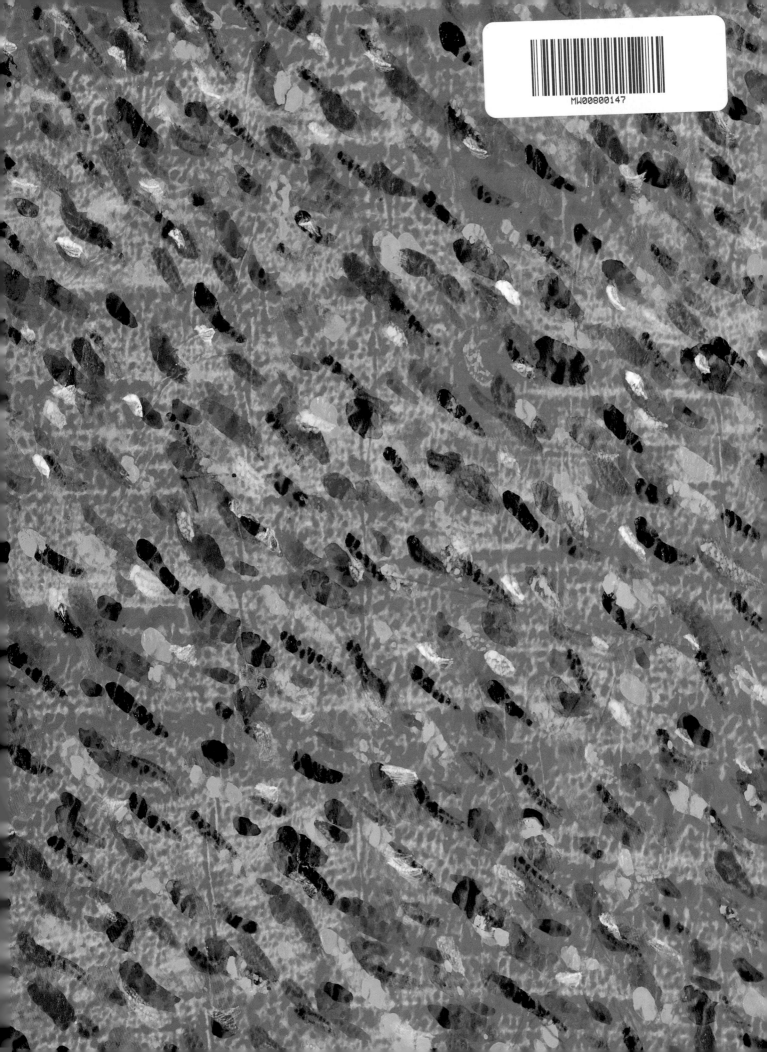

Tom Thumb

Grimms' Tales

retold and illustrated by Eric Carle

Orchard Books   **An Imprint of Scholastic Inc.**   **New York**

Library of Congress Cataloging-in-Publication Data
Carle, Eric.
Tom Thumb: Grimms' tales / retold and illustrated by Eric Carle. —1st ed.
v. cm.
"The stories in this newly released collection of Grimms' tales were originally published by Orchard Books in *Eric Carle's treasury of classic stories for children*"—T.p. verso. "Portions of this book appeared in *Eric Carle's storybook: seven tales by the Brothers Grimm*, retold and illustrated by Eric Carle, published in 1976 by Franklin Watts, New York, New York"—T.p. verso.
Contents: Tom Thumb — The fisherman and his wife — Hans in luck — The seven Swabians.
ISBN 978-0-545-27009-0
1. Fairy tales—Germany. [1. Fairy tales. 2. Folklore—Germany.] I. Grimm, Jacob, 1785–1863. II. Grimm, Wilhelm, 1786–1859.
III. Carle, Eric. *Eric Carle's treasury of classic stories for children*. IV. Carle, Eric. *Eric Carle's storybook*. V. Title.

PZ8.C214To 2011
398.2—dc22 [E]

2010042723

10 9 8 7 6 5 4 3 2 1   11 12 13 14 15
Printed in Singapore 46
First edition, October 2011

For Nadja and Teresa

Contents

Tom Thumb 11

The Fisherman and His Wife 23

Hans in Luck 33

The Seven Swabians 47

Tom Thumb

A poor woodcutter sat by the fire one evening, while his wife sat across from him, spinning. He said, "What a sad thing it is that we have no children. We live too quietly. A child would cheer us up."

"Yes," said his wife. "I'd even be glad of one the size of my thumb."

Some time later they had a son, and sure enough, he was no bigger than a thumb. They named him Tom Thumb, and they loved him dearly and gave him the best of care.

Time passed. Tom never grew any larger, but he was strong and healthy. He became a quick, bright child who did well at whatever he tried.

One morning, when his father was getting ready to go into the forest to cut some wood, he said, "I wish I had someone to bring me the horse and cart later on."

"Leave the horse to me," said Tom. "I can bring him."

"Very well," replied his father.

That afternoon Tom climbed up and sat between the horse's ears. "Gittup," he called to the horse in a big brave voice, and away they went together.

Two strangers were passing through the woods and saw the horse galloping. They heard Tom calling to it to turn right or left, but there was no one to be seen. "That's very strange," they said. "Let's follow the cart and see what happens when it stops."

Soon the men came to the spot where Tom's father was waiting, and they hid behind a tree.

"Here I am, Father," Tom called. "Didn't I drive the horse well?"

"Yes, you're a fine boy," said the woodcutter, as he lifted Tom to his shoulder.

"We could make a fortune with that odd little fellow," said one of the men. "If we showed him in the towns for money, people would pay to see him. Let's buy him."

"Hey, there," he said to the woodcutter. "Here's a fine piece of gold. Sell us the boy. We'll take good care of him."

"No," said the woodcutter. "He is all my wife and I have, and we love him with all our hearts."

But Tom whispered in his father's ear, "Take the gold and don't worry about me. I'll be home before you know it."

"Well, all right then," said the woodcutter, and he took the gold.

One of the men put Tom on the rim of his hat and they all said their good-byes. Tom's father went one way with the horse and the wood and the piece of gold. The two men went the other way with Tom riding on the hat.

After a while, Tom called, "Let me down."

"No," said the men. "You'll just run away."

"But it's important business," said Tom.

So the men put Tom down in the grass. Quick as a wink he ran into a mouse hole. "Good-bye, gentlemen," he called.

The men looked everywhere, but they could not see Tom. They poked in the hole, but he stayed safely out of reach. "We've been tricked," they said angrily, and they went on their way.

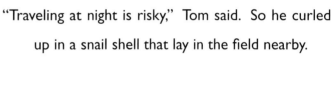

When Tom came out of the hole, the moon was up. "Traveling at night is risky," Tom said. So he curled up in a snail shell that lay in the field nearby.

Just as he was falling asleep, he heard two men passing by.

"That rich man has gold and silver and jewels, but how can we get in to steal them?" asked one man.

"I can help you," shouted Tom.

"Whose voice is that? Where are you?" asked the thieves.

"Here. In the grass."

When the thieves saw Tom, they laughed.

"How could a little fellow like you help us?" they said.

"I could slip into the house and hand out to you whatever you want," said Tom.

"All right, it's worth a try," said the thieves. "Come along."

But when Tom got inside the house, he called out in a loud voice, "What do you want? Shall I hand out everything?"

"S-sh," said the thieves. "Not so loud."

Tom pretended not to understand.

"Hold out your hands," he shouted. "Here's some gold."

The maid heard the noise and came with a lamp. Quickly the thieves ran away, and Tom, pleased with himself, tiptoed out to the barn. There he went to sleep in a pile of soft hay, thinking he'd be home in time for dinner the next day. In the morning the maid came to feed the cow. She picked up the pile of hay where Tom was sleeping. When he woke up, he was in the cow's mouth. The cow swallowed, and Tom slid into her stomach. He screamed, but the maid had already left to do the baking.

Later the maid came back to milk the cow. Imagine her surprise when she heard a voice inside it, crying, "Let me out. Let me out."

She ran to her master. "The cow is talking," she said.

Her master came to listen. Again a voice called, "Let me out. Let me out."

The master turned pale with fright. "It's an evil spirit," he said. "We must kill the cow."

So he butchered the cow and threw her stomach into the rubbish heap, with Tom still inside. Tom twisted and turned, trying to work his way out of the stomach. Just as he was beginning to sniff fresh air a starving wolf came by. The wolf pounced on the stomach and gulped it down—but still Tom did not lose courage.

"Dear friend," called Tom from inside the wolf, "I know where you can find the most delicious food."

"Where is that?" asked the wolf.

"The woodcutter's house," said Tom. "I'll tell you how to get there."

When they came to the house, Tom said, "Go to the narrow window in the back, and force yourself through. That's where the pantry is."

The wolf pushed his way through the narrow window and ate until he was stuffed full. But when he tried to leave, his stomach had grown so big and fat he could not get out.

Now Tom began to scream as loud as he could, "Help, help!"

"Be quiet," said the wolf. "You'll wake everyone up." But Tom kept on screaming.

Before long, the woodcutter and his wife heard the noise and came with an ax. Upon seeing the wolf, the woodcutter shouted, "I'll get you, you thief!" And he swung the ax back for the kill.

"Father, Father!" yelled Tom. "I'm in the wolf's belly."

"Don't worry, I won't hurt you," the woodcutter replied, and he struck the wolf dead with one blow on its head. Then he cut the wolf open and took Tom out. "Thank heaven you're back," he said. "Where on earth have you been?"

"I've been seeing the world," said Tom. "Now I am happy to breathe the fresh air again. I've been inside a mouse hole, a snail shell, a cow's stomach, and a wolf's belly. And now I'll stay right here with you."

"And we will never give you away again for all the gold in the world," said his parents, as they hugged and kissed their child.

The Fisherman and His Wife

There was once a poor fisherman who lived with his wife in a tiny hut by the sea. Each morning he went down to the shore and cast his net for fish. One day he pulled up a fish with gold and silver scales. "Oh," said the fish, "I beg you to let me go. I am really an enchanted prince, and not at all good to eat."

"Prince or no prince, any fish who can talk has earned its freedom," said the fisherman, and he let the fish go.

When he told his wife what had happened, she said, "You nincompoop, that was a magic fish, the kind that makes wishes come true. You should have made a wish."

"But we have everything we need," said the fisherman.

His wife did not listen. "Tomorrow," she said, "catch the fish again and ask it for a big house like those in the city. And I'd like a black dress with white frills, too."

The fisherman did not like to oppose his wife so he cast his net in the same place the next day. Little waves were beating against the shore. Soon he pulled up the fish. "What is it?" asked the fish with the silver and gold scales.

"My wife says I should have made a wish," said the fisherman. "She wants a big house like those in the city, and a black dress with white frills."

"Go home," said the fish. "She has them already."

The fisherman went home. Sure enough, his wife, in a black dress with white frills, stood in front of a big house.

A week passed, and the fisherman's wife began to find the house too small. "Find the magic fish," she said. "I want to be a queen and live in a castle."

"But surely now we have everything we need," said the fisherman.

"I must be queen," his wife kept saying. Finally the fisherman gave in and went to the water.

The water along the shore was black, and the wind was high. The fisherman said to the fish when it appeared, "My wife wants to be queen and live in a castle."

"Go home," said the fish. "She already has her wish."

The fisherman went home and, indeed, his wife was now a queen. She stood at the door of a splendid big castle.

"Ah," said the fisherman. "Now you are queen. There is nothing more you can want."

"I am not satisfied with being queen," said his wife. "Go to the fish and tell it I want to be pope."

"Oh, no," said the fisherman. "This time you are asking too much. I do not want to go."

But in the end he went to find the fish. The waves were as high as mountains, and the sky was black. In fright, the fisherman said, "My wife now wants to be pope."

"Go home," said the fish. "She has her wish."

The fisherman went home and found a great church decorated in gold. Tall candles burned before his wife, who was dressed in a pope's robes.

"Now surely you cannot wish for anything more," he said.

"I will think about it," replied his wife. That night she could not sleep, thinking of what else she might be. She got up early, just as the sun was rising. "Ah," she thought, "I should like to be the one who makes the sun rise."

She awoke her husband. "Go to the fish," she commanded. "Tell it I want to make the sun rise. I want to be ruler of the universe."

In terror, the fisherman went to the shore. A wild storm was raging. "Oh, fish," shouted the fisherman above the noise of the wind, "my wife wants to be ruler of the universe."

"Go home," said the fish. And the fisherman went home. He found his wife dressed in her old clothes inside their little hut.

For the rest of their lives the fisherman and his wife lived in the little hut by the sea. Every day the fisherman went to the shore and cast his net. As the years went by, he pulled up hundreds of fish, but never again did he see the magic gold- and silver-scaled fish who could talk and grant wishes.

Hans in Luck

Hans had worked seven years with a miller and he felt it was time to go home.

"Seven years have passed, and that is long enough," he said to his master one morning. "I would like to see my mother. Please give me my wages, and I'll be on my way."

"Hans," said the miller, "you have been a good and faithful worker. My wife and I shall miss you, but we wish you the best of luck and a safe trip home."

The miller went to his strongbox and took out Hans's wages. "Here is your pay," he said, and gave Hans a piece of gold the size of his head.

Hans wrapped the gold inside a sack and threw it over his shoulder. He took his walking stick in his hand, crossed the bridge to the road, and started on his way home.

The road was rough and hilly, and the mid-morning sun was hot. Hans began to sweat. The gold seemed very heavy indeed. Just then a horseman came galloping by.

"Ah," said Hans, "a horse is a fine thing. A horseman does not have to carry a heavy load like mine on his back."

"What is in your sack?" asked the horseman.

"It is a piece of gold, and it is quite a lump to carry," said Hans.

"If you like, we will trade," said the horseman. "I will give you the horse and you will give me the gold."

"A good deal," said Hans.

The man helped Hans onto the horse, then made off with the gold as fast as he could. Hans went on his way, feeling lucky to be riding along so easily. But the horse soon understood that Hans was no rider, and Hans was thrown to the ground. A farmer milking his cow in a nearby field stopped the horse and helped Hans to his feet.

Hans was very thirsty. "Dear man," he said to the farmer, "it must be wonderful to have milk whenever you want some. And good fresh butter and cheese, besides. How I would like to have a cow."

"A cow is indeed a very fine thing," replied the farmer, "but a horse can be useful too. If you like, I will trade my cow for your horse."

"A good deal," said Hans. "A horse is not for me. I will never ride that animal again. A cow will suit me better." He took the cow, and the farmer climbed onto the horse and rode away in a great hurry.

Hans felt he was the luckiest man in the world, and he sat down to milk his cow. But milking a cow was something he had never done before and he was clumsy at it. He pushed and pinched and pulled, but the cow would give no milk. Hans tried again, twice as hard. At last the cow became impatient. She raised one of her hind legs and gave Hans a good kick.

Just then it happened that a man was passing by on the road. He had a big fat pig, which he was taking to market.

"Why should the cow kick you?" asked the man.

Hans told of his troubles. "The cow looks poorly," said the man. "Maybe she doesn't give much milk."

"What?" said Hans. "How much better if I had a lovely fat pig like yours. Pork chops and roasts, to say nothing of sausages."

"Well," said the man, "just for you, I'll trade. You take the pig and I'll take the cow."

The exchange was made and Hans set out again. But the pig was stubborn. No matter how much Hans wanted to go one way, the pig wanted to go the other way. Besides, it squealed and screeched and grunted like—well, just like a pig.

Hans was getting discouraged when a woman with a fat goose walked by.

"Eggs for breakfast," Hans thought, "and feathers for a pillow, and a roast for Christmas, all from one bird. Not bad. Perhaps the woman is willing to trade."

The woman knew a good bargain when she saw one and was happy to trade. Hans went on and was close to home when he saw a knife grinder at work. What fun! Sparks were flying through the air, and the grinder's money pouch was full of coins.

"That's a fine goose you have," said the grinder. "Where did you buy it?"

"It was a lucky swap," said Hans, and he told the grinder of all his trades, starting with the lump of gold.

"You've a good head for business," said the grinder. "You should take up my work."

"How can I do that?" said Hans. "I have no grindstone."

"Well," said the grinder, as he picked up a loose cobblestone from the road. "It so happens that I have an extra one. I'll trade it, just for the goose." And so they traded a goose for the old cobblestone.

Hans felt he was the luckiest man in the world. But he had walked a long way and he was very tired and thirsty. The stone grew heavier and heavier every minute. At last he came to a water fountain. He put the stone at the fountain's edge and bent over to take a drink. The stone rolled over and sank deep into the water with a loud *plump*.

Hans laughed. "How lucky I am," he said. "Now I am free, with nothing at all to carry anymore."

And he ran home, where his mother saw him coming and rushed to greet him. "Oh, Hans, how I have missed you," said his mother. "How wonderful it is to have you home again."

She gave him a big warm hug and led him to the most comfortable chair in the house so that he could sit and rest. Then she bustled around, telling him all the village news while she prepared his favorite supper, a dish of steaming dumplings. Now, more than ever, Hans felt that he was the luckiest young man in the world.

The Seven Swabians

There were once seven Swabians who went out to see the world hoping for adventure and the chance to perform brave deeds. For protection they took just one long spear. After days of marching, at last they had their chance. In the middle of a field, they saw a creature sitting with its big eyes wide open and its big ears pricked up. The Swabians had never seen a rabbit before and they thought it was a monster. They lined up along their spear when fear overcame them. Instead of attacking, they cried for mercy.

Only the small Swabian, at the end of the spear's handle, kept pushing—he could not see the rabbit. The others fled in all directions to hide, and the rabbit ran away. When the Swabians thought things safe, they crept out of hiding.

They lined up again, grasping their spear, and started marching again. Soon they came to a wide river. There was no bridge across it and there were no boats. A man was working on the other side, and the Swabians called to him, "How can we get across?" He did not understand them, so he called back, "What? What?"

The Swabians thought he was saying, "Wade. Wade." So the leader walked into the water, followed by the other Swabians, each in his place, marching left right, left right, into the river—all except the little one at the end. As usual, he was not paying attention. The six valiant Swabians soon sank to the bottom. When the smallest Swabian saw the leader's hat bobbing along the river, he knew that something was wrong, and returned home to tell this story.

About the Brothers Grimm

The brothers Grimm, Wilhelm (1786–1859) and Jacob (1785–1863), were linguists and scholars who worked harmoniously as a team throughout their lives. After the classicism and restraints of the eighteenth century there had come a desire not only for beauty but also for strangeness and mystery, and out of this was born the Romantic movement in literature. The folk and fairy stories the Grimms collected from the common people near their home in Hesse, Germany, were published in 1812–1824. Their immediate popularity may have surprised the serious brothers, but with their elves, dwarves, and talking animals of the forest, their peasants and princesses, they fitted the Romantic mode perfectly. They were translated and published in England in 1823–1826, with illustrations by George Cruikshank, where they were read and enjoyed by adults and children alike.

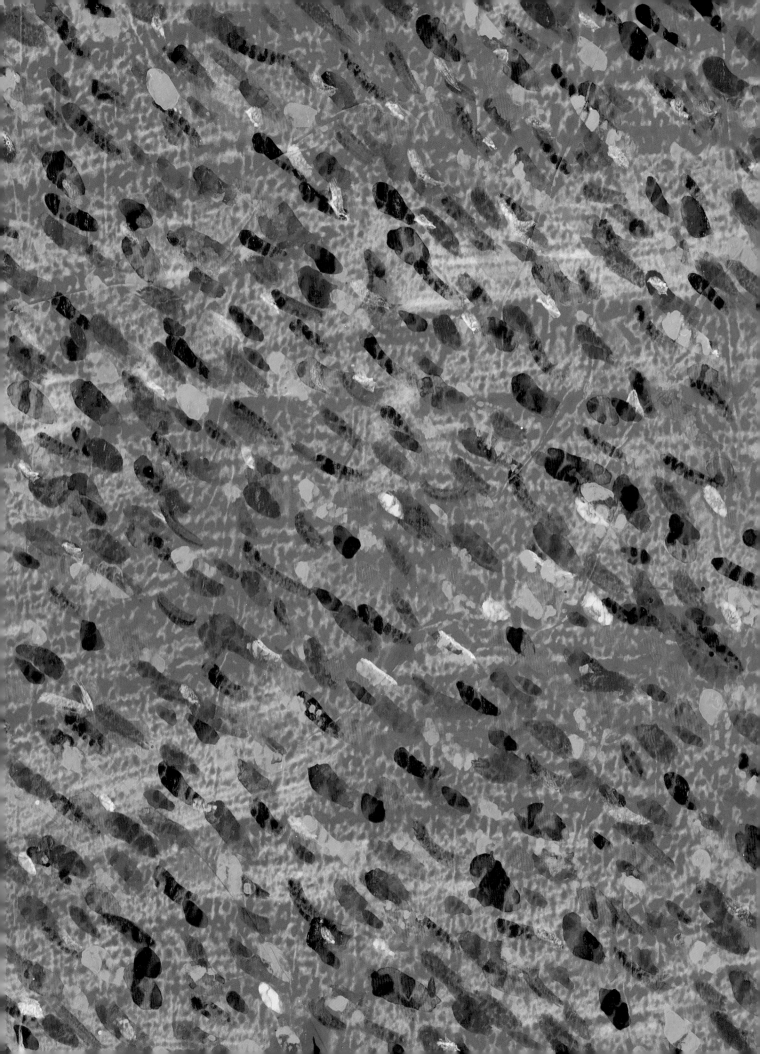